Raj in Charge

Andrew and Diana Davies

Illustrated by
Debi Gliori

PUFFIN BOOKS

PUFFIN BOOKS

Published by the Penguin Group
Penguin Books Ltd, 27 Wrights Lane, London W8 5TZ, England
Penguin Books USA Inc., 375 Hudson Street, New York, New York 10014, USA
Penguin Books Australia Ltd, Ringwood, Victoria, Australia
Penguin Books Canada Ltd, 10 Alcorn Avenue, Toronto, Ontario, Canada M4V 3B2
Penguin Books (NZ) Ltd, 182–190 Wairau Road, Auckland 10, New Zealand

Penguin Books Ltd, Registered Offices: Harmondsworth, Middlesex, England

First published by Hamish Hamilton Ltd 1994
Published in Puffin Books 1996
7 9 10 8 6

Text copyright © Andrew and Diana Davies, 1994
Illustrations copyright © Debi Gliori, 1994
All rights reserved

The moral right of the authors and illustrator has been asserted

Filmset in Plantin

Printed in Hong Kong by Midas Printing Limited

PUFFIN BOOKS

Raj in Charge

Raj was always in trouble.

He was not a very bad boy, but he did
have this urge to muck about with things.
He got on everybody's nerves in Class Two,
and Mrs Turnip had to tell him off every
day.

One Monday he let out Henry the guinea pig for a game of Jump The Pencil.

"Miss! Miss! Raji's let Henry out!" shouted Annette and Gurpal.

"Raj! Put him back this minute!" said
Mrs Turnip.

"I'm not hurting him," said Raj.
"Henry's my friend. I'm training him to be
a great jumper."

"You are mucking about again, Raj."

"Sorry, Mrs Turnip."
"Well, stop it then."
"Yes, Mrs Turnip."

But he couldn't stop it.

At story time, just when Mrs Turnip had got to a very quiet whispery bit of the story, he crept up to the gong and gave it a great loud BONG! Everyone jumped, and Mrs Turnip fell off the story chair.

"Oh, *Raj*!" said Mrs Turnip. "What on earth was that for?"

"Music, Mrs Turnip. You know, to go with the story."

"Mucking about again, Raj. Stop it."

"Yes, Mrs Turnip."

But he couldn't stop it. He couldn't stop
mucking about. At lunch time he hid
Linford's lunch in the dressing-up box.

In the afternoon he broke four pencils.
(He said he was very sorry and he must be
much stronger than he thought.) And just
before home time he let Henry the guinea
pig out again.

"Well, he kept looking at me," said Raj.
It took a long time to catch Henry.

"Raj," said Mrs Turnip. "I am a patient woman but enough is enough. Things must change. Now listen very carefully, all of you. From tomorrow, I am going to put Raj in charge."

Everybody in Class Two was flabbergasted. What could Mrs Turnip mean?

"Raj," she said. "From tomorrow, it's your job to make sure that:

no one breaks the pencils

no one bangs the gong in story time

no one hides lunchboxes

and no one lets the guinea pig out.

It's a very big job for just one boy. Do you think you can do it?"

"Yes, Mrs Turnip," said Raj. "Easy peasy."

Everybody fell about laughing. Raj in charge? Big joke!

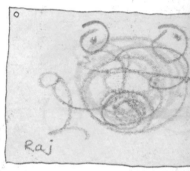

But the next day, Raj came to school very early with a serious look on his face.

"Linford and Floella! Put those lunchboxes there in the corner where I can see them," he said.

"And don't go near Henry's cage, please, Georgina. Careful with the pencils, Sam."

"Leave the gong alone in story time, we mustn't frighten Mrs Turnip. And no mucking about, because Raj is in charge. OK?"

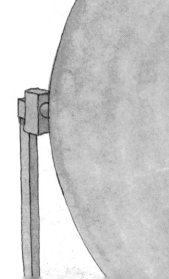

And all that day, there was no mucking about. Nobody broke any pencils or hid anybody else's lunch, and Henry the guinea pig had a very quiet, peaceful day.

"Well done, Raji," said Mrs Turnip at
the end of the afternoon.

And Raj went home very pleased with himself. He felt very tired, though. His big brother and sister had got an exciting video with robbers and space monsters and Giant Sumatran Rats, but Raj felt so tired that after supper he went straight up to bed and straight to sleep.

In the middle of the night he woke up
feeling worried. What if someone got into
the school in the night and mucked about?
Robbers might come and steal Henry the
guinea pig! Space monsters might come and
rampage about in the book corner and the
dressing-up box! Giant Sumatran Rats
might come and chew up the pencils!
Anything might happen. And Raj was in
charge.

He got up and crept downstairs.
Everything was quiet. He tiptoed round the
house and he found:
his big brother's loud silver whistle
his big sister's karate headband
his dad's old hockey stick
and his mum's big heavy torch
and a two pound bag of biscuits.

Then he went to school, all on his own in the middle of the night.

He was only just in time. He had hardly settled down on some cushions in the book corner when six robbers crept in through the classroom door!

"Police! Inspector Raj in charge!"
shouted Raj, and he shone his torch and
blew his big brother's whistle as loud as he
could. The robbers were so terrified they
dived head first out of the window.

Next came three Space Monsters who had been hiding in the cupboard.

They were heading for the book corner
when Raj jumped out of the dressing-up box
in his sister's headband, whirling his dad's
hockey stick around his head. The Space
Monsters went pale and scurried back into
the cupboard, and Raj turned the key in the
lock.

He was having a little rest and eating one
or two biscuits when he heard loud snuffles
at the door, and the chomping of huge furry
jaws. It was the Sumatran Rats. They had
come for the pencils. One by one they
shuffled into Mrs Turnip's dark classroom.

"Look," said Raj wearily. "I'm tired of all this mucking about. Eating pencils is stupid. If I give you these biscuits will you go home?"

The giant rats looked at each other, then held out their paws for the biscuits. Then one by one they shuffled out of the school, never to be seen again.

Outside it was just beginning to get light. Raj had saved the school. It was time to go home.

Next morning, Mrs Turnip said, "Raji! Are you all right? You look as if you haven't slept all night!"

"It's that job," said Raj. "It's too tiring, being in charge of everything. Can't I go back to just being in charge of myself?"

Mrs Turnip looked at him. He did look tired.

"Yes," she said. "All right. But no mucking about. Promise?"

"Well," said Raj. "I'll try."

WHAT STELLA SAW
Wendy Smith

Stella's mum is a fortune-teller who always gets things wrong. But when football-mad Stella starts reading tea leaves, she seems to be right every time! Or is she . . .

THE DAY THE SMELLS WENT WRONG
Catherine Sefton

It is just an ordinary day, but Jackie and Phil can't understand why nothing smells as it should. Toast smells like tar, fruit smells like fish, and their school dinners smell of perfume!
Together, Jackie and Phil discover the cause of the problem . . .

BELLA AT THE BALLET
Brian Ball

Bella has been looking forward to her first ballet lesson for ages – but she's cross when Mum says Baby Tommy is coming with them. Bella is sure Tommy will spoil everything, but in the end it's hard to know who enjoys the class more – Bella or Tommy!